There's a Tiger In My

Sarah Froggatt

First published in Singapore and UK on 22nd March 2016
LimeyLimericks Publishing in association Discover English
and CreateSpace

ISBN 13: Soft Cover 978-1530443147

ISBN 10: 1530443148

www.limeylimericks.com
www.discoverenglish.education

For Mimi and Colette

Foreword

In November 2014, residents of a suburb of Paris reported seeing a tiger lurking around the neighbourhood.

Everyone wondered where it had come from, and moreover, where it was going. Maybe it was lonely and looking for friends?

I think I know.

Teaching poetry at both primary and secondary grades, I have come to realise how our education systems work to decimate any love of poetry that children hold. My desire is to change that.

Poetry is music; it stimulates the same part of the brain as music: the right hemisphere; and at the same time, it stimulates imagination, vocabulary and creative thinking. How cool is that for children and adults alike?

Out of a poem, a waterfall of magic pours; it creates an enchanting world where rhythm, rhyme and tone encourage laughter, reading, writing and speaking. What could be more fantastic than that?

All children should have the chance to love poetry, to learn at least one poem that they will cherish forever, and to be able to recite it with fond memories.

Who knows, one day this tiger might just be one of them.

There's a Tiger In My House

Acknowledgements:

BBC (2014) 'Paris tiger': Big cat loose near french capital - report. Available at: http://www.bbc.com/news/world-europe-30035666 (Accessed: 13 November 2014).

Packwood, R. and gettyimages (no date) Tiger videos, photos and facts - Panthera tigris. Available at: http://www.arkive.org/tiger/panthera-tigris/ (Accessed: 16 March 2016).

Society, N.G. (2014) Tiger. Available at: http://kids.nationalgeographic.com/animals/tiger/#tiger-swimming.jpg (Accessed: 16 March 2016).

Fonts: Divide by Zero user profile: 1001 fonts (no date) Available at: http://www.1001fonts.com/users/tom7/ (Accessed: 10 February 2016).

HElp!

There's a tiger

prowling in my street,

I saw his huge
and stripy feet!

He padded quietly
on all fours,

Leaving marks of tiger paws.

He flicked his tail and looked at me,

Then turned and hid behind a
tree.

Help!

There's a tiger in my garden,

He came in without a pardon.

He's hiding ...

in amongst the flowers,

Looking
for his
super powers!
Waiting,
till I turn my
back,
I hope
I'm not
his
morning
snack!

HElp!

There's a tiger behind the wall,

I saw his shadow, dark and tall.

Waiting for a moment to pounce,

Or surprise me,

with an uber bounce.

Now I know he's following me,

I'll hide inside,

where

he

can't

see.

Help!

There's a
tiger
inside
my house,

He crept in, silent, like a
mOuse.

He's exploring everything inside,

Searching for a place to hide.

Now, he's hiding behind the door,

I see his toes,

I'm really sure!

I need to save my teddy  bears.

I saw him turn his ear to hear,

If anything to eat was near.

I need to keep my teddies

quiet,

And not part of his hungry

diet.

HeLp!

There's a tiger on the stair rail,

I'm sure I saw his *claws* and tail.

He left a huge, ginormous scratch,

My nails could never, ever match.

I need to hide my

toys,

away,

This tiger's just not here to play.

HeLp!

There's a tiger under all my clothes,

I saw his shiny, wet, pink nose.

It twitched,

and sniffed,

a bit at me,

I felt it brush against my knee!

I'm sure he wants to take my

tOys,

I better not make any noise!

HeLp!

I saw his teeth all sharp,

His hungry jaws gaped far apart,

His long white whiskers tickled me,

As I froze and waited

silently.

I didn't know

if I'd stay

awake,

I didn't know

how I'd

escape.

Help!

There's a **tiger** underneath my bed,

I saw his whiskers and his head.

His beady eyes shone out at

me,

He licked and smacked

his chops in glee.

I shone my torch

there,

just in case,

To get a glimpse of his

cheeky face.

And then,   my eyes

                    began to close,
And, I fell into a nighttime doze.

        I dreamt the

        tiger

had come to stay,

Not to eat,

but just to play.

But when I woke,

with a big

yawn

The tiger'd left

before the

dawn.

And now he's left,

and gone back home,

Leaving me, and my toys alone.

Mum said it was all just a dream.

But I know what I'd heard and seen.

There had been

a

tiger

In my house,

creeping

and

sneaking

like

a

MOUSE.

Tiger Facts

The tiger is the largest wild cat in the world. The tiger's tail can measure up to 1 meter long. Tigers are the only striped wild cat.

There are nine sub-species, but three became extinct by the end of 20th Century. The Sumatran tiger is the smallest of the sub-species, and has the darkest coat.

Tigers coats range from a reddish-orange to yellow-ochre colour, their belly is white and their stripes are black. The black stripes are unique to each cat, some are single, some at various spaces and some with double stripes.

The tiger is a solitary creature and usually hunts alone. They wait until after dark to hunt and then pounce on their prey.

Tigers are unusual as they like water and can swim well.

Tigers live in a wide range of habitats, from tropical forests, jungles, swamps and grasslands. Unfortunately, many of their habitats are under threat as humans take away land for farming and logging.

Tigers are extremely endangered. They have been overhunted for their fur and body parts that some countries continue to use for traditional medicine.

About the Author

Story telling and writing has been a passion since I was young. My father told me stories about two naughty monkeys named Hoko and Poko who lived amongst the banana trees in Jamaica, when I could not sleep at night.

His mother had told him the same tales.

When my boys were younger, I created adventures for my own two cheeky monkeys. Encouraging my boys to join in; sometimes we would end up on a wild chase across Antarctica or falling into some mysterious land.

As a child, I loved illustrated stories: often disappointed whenever I picked up a book that did not have a picture or an image. I am still mesmerised when I read the fairy tales and Arabian Nights illustrated by Edmund Dulac, or Quentin Blake's illustrations of Roald Dahl stories and Chris Riddell's Gothic creations.

I hand illustrate my books - they are an extension of the words and ideas in my head.

I could never imagine a world without books and stories, and art. My true wish is that children, everywhere, will continue to read and love books for all eternity.

Animal Tails Mayan Cocoa

The Balloon Ride Rotten Eggs

Leopard Spots

Rhino Itch My Curious Brain of Noise

Orangutan Swing

Artful Art & Friends  Eric and the Volcano

Made in the USA
Charleston, SC
31 March 2016